JANE KEMP and CLARE WALTERS have worked together
as a writing team for many years. They are the co-authors
of many children's books, as well as a number of books for parents,
many of which have been published internationally.
They have also been scriptwriters for the highly successful
BBC children's television series *Balamory* and *Me Too!*
Jane and Clare formerly worked on the respected babycare publication
Practical Parenting and still work in the magazine industry.
Their previous books for Frances Lincoln include
I Very Really Miss You, illustrated by Jonathan Langley,
Mum Mine and *Dad Mine*, and *Cat* and *Dog*.

PENNY DALE studied Fine Art and Design at Exeter College of Art,
and has worked on community arts projects, stage design and as
a graphic designer. She had her first book published in 1986.
Since then, she has written and illustrated many books,
including stories by Martin Waddell and Anne Fine.
Her books have been published in over twenty languages.
Penny won the Best Books for Babies Award for *Rosie's Babies*
by Martin Waddell, and has also been shortlisted twice for the
Kate Greenway Medal. This is her first book for Frances Lincoln.

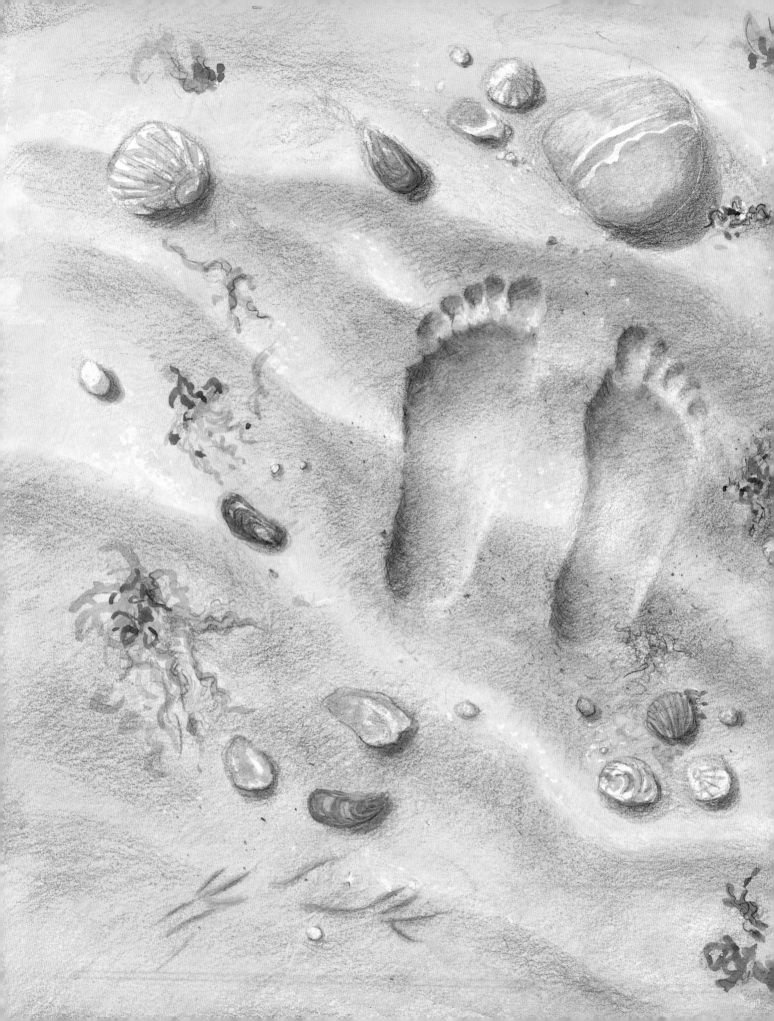

For Richard – *J.K.*
For Jessica and Rosie – *C.W.*
For Jenny, Ella and Sam – *P. D.*

First published in Great Britain in 2006 and in the USA in 2007
by Frances Lincoln Children's Books, 4 Torriano Mews,
Torriano Avenue, London NW5 2RZ

www.franceslincoln.com

First paperback edition published in Great Britain in 2008 and in the USA in 2009

British Library Cataloguing in Publication Data available on request

ISBN 978-1-84507-618-4

Printed in Singapore

1 3 5 7 9 8 6 4 2

Time to Say I Love You

Jane Kemp & Clare Walters
Illustrated by **Penny Dale**

F
FRANCES LINCOLN
CHILDREN'S BOOKS

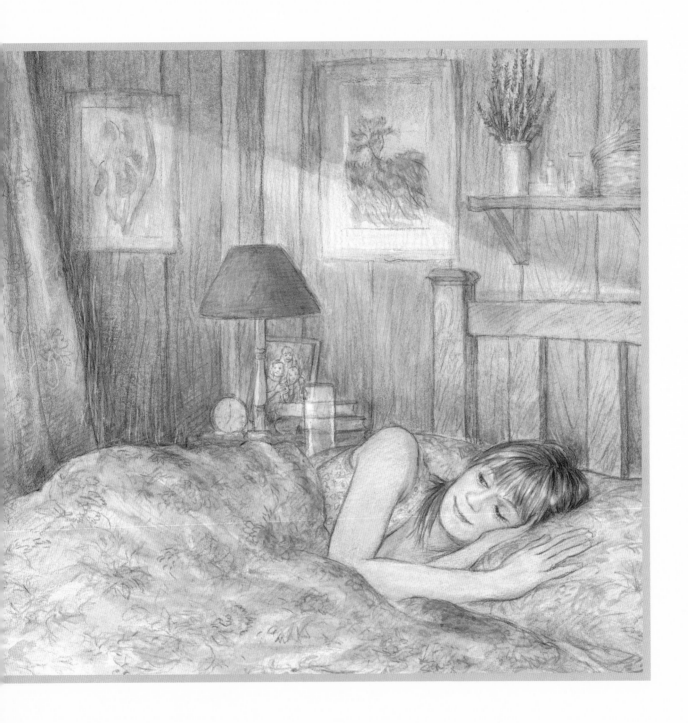

When's the best time to say I love you?

Shall I say it when you wake me with a kiss?

Shall I say it when you're
riding tall upon my shoulders?

Shall I say it when we're
chasing waves across the sand?

Shall I say it when we're climbing high up on the hill?

Shall I say it when we're
painting pictures in the clouds?

Shall I say it when we're
dashing homewards through the rain?

Shall I say it when we're curled up close
beside the fire?

Shall I say it when we're gazing at the stars?

When is the best time to say I love you?

Right now. I LOVE YOU!

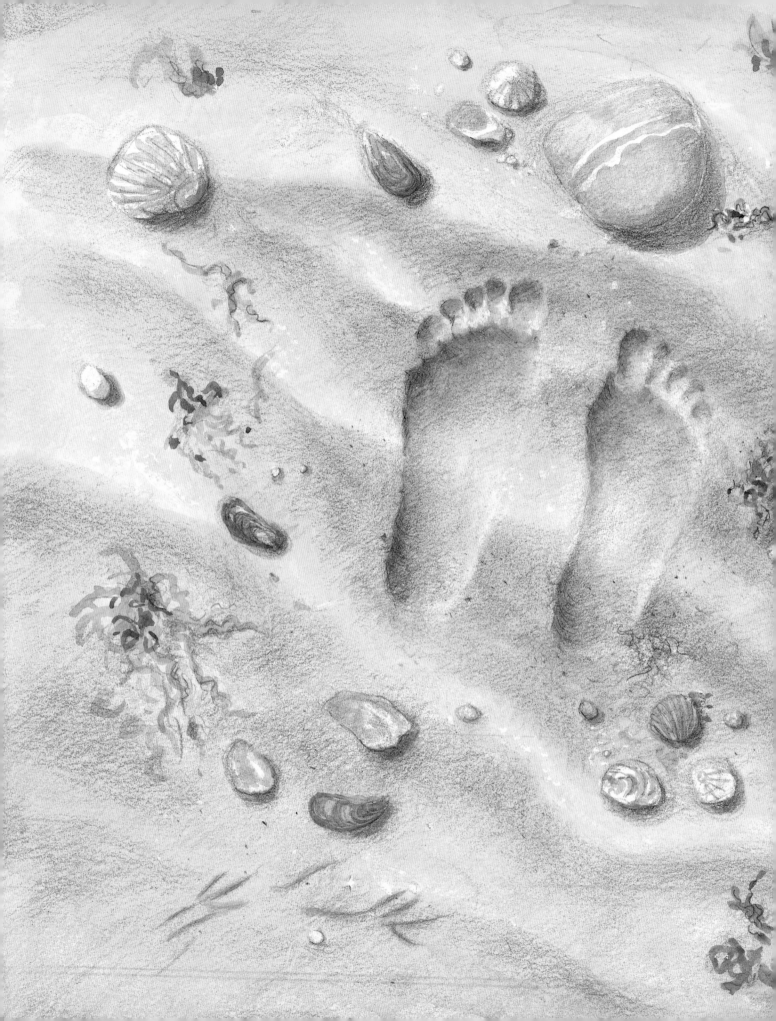

MORE TITLES FROM FRANCES LINCOLN CHILDREN'S BOOKS

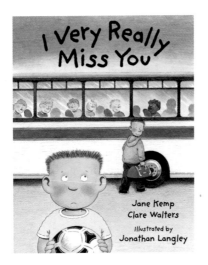

I Very Really Miss You
Jane Kemp and Clare Walters
Illustrated by Jonathan Langley

Sam's big brother Ben is going away on a school trip for one whole week – and Sam is glad. Because for one whole week he can play with all the toys, have the whole bedroom to himself and he won't get squirted by Ben's water pistol. But it is too quiet without Ben and Sam starts to miss his big brother. So Sam writes Ben a postcard to say he very really misses him and he is surprised to learn that Ben very really missed him too!

Seven For a Secret
Laurence Anholt
Illustrated by Jim Coplestone

Ruby lives in the city and Grandpa lives in the country. They write to each other and share the events in their lives. Ruby tells about the flights of stairs in their apartment block and the sights of the city. Grampa tells Ruby about the naughty magpies that live in his old oak tree. Through the Magpie Song, the events of the story unravel – three magpies for Ruby the magpie girl, one for a heart-breaking goodbye and six for a wonderful surprise that will change Ruby's life forever.

A Kiss Like This
Catherine and Laurence Anholt

Everyone needs kisses. Tickly monkey kisses, slurpy sloppy elephant kisses, even snippy snappy crocodile kisses. But when you are a sleepy Little Lion Cub, the only kiss that's just right is a huge great Big Golden Lion kiss – just like this!

Frances Lincoln titles are available from all good bookshops.
You can also buy books and find out more about your favourite titles,
authors and illustrators on our website: www.franceslincoln.com